SANKEY

❧ THE SINGER AND HIS SONG ❧

SANKEY

THE SINGER AND HIS SONG

Helen Rothwell

AMBASSADOR

Belfast • Greenville

First published 1946

Copyright © 1996 Ambassador Productions Ltd.

ISBN 1 898787 64 6

Published by

AMBASSADOR PRODUCTIONS, LTD.
Providence House
16 Hillview Avenue,
Belfast, BT5 6JR

Emerald House
1 Chick Springs Road, Suite 102
Greenville, South Carolina, 29609

Printed in Northern Ireland

CONTENTS

1

"FROM A CHILD THOU HAST KNOWN"

II Timothy 3:15

D estined to become the sweet singer of Methodism who should waft the message of salvation to the hearts of millions on the wings of song, Ira David Sankey was born in the small village of Edinburgh, in Lawrence County, Western Pennsylvania, on the twenty-eighth day of August, 1840. His parents, David and Mary Sankey, the former of English and the latter of Scotch-Irish descent, were pious Methodists who knew how to make home happy for their nine children and at the same time bring them up in the fear of the Lord.

Young David learned his first hymn from the lips of his sweet-voiced mother, who quited him with the strains of a tender lullaby. One of his chief boyhood pleasures was to join the family circle about the great log fireplace, where they spent the long winter evenings singing the grand old hymns of the church. In this way the youthful singer learned to read music so that he, by the age of eight, could sing correctly many famous hymn tunes. His cheerful spirit and his early interest in music were a delight to all the family.

David's earliest recollection of spiritual matters revolved around a certain Mr. Fraser who loved children intensely and who took the young boy, along with his own sons, to the Sunday school held in the old schoolhouse. There the sweetness of his voice and his pleasant manner won for David a place of esteem and admiration. Qualities of leadership early asserted themselves, and David became an acknowledged leader among his boyhood associates.

Since Mr. Sankey was a man of considerable importance in the community in which he lived, having held various offices of honour, he was able to give his son educational opportunities that were above the average in his day. In 1857 the family moved to the growing city of Newcastle, where Mr. Sankey assumed the presidency of the bank and David attended high school. Later he took a position in the bank. Shortly before his removal to Newcastle David had been brought under deep conviction for his sins and had been converted while attending revival meetings at a church known as The King's Chapel, located about three miles from his home. At Newcastle he became a member of the Methodist Episcopal Church, were his spirituality, ability for leadership and musical talents were soon recognised, for he was elected superintendent of the Sunday school, director of the choir, and subsequently a class leader.

In training the members of his choir young Sankey gained much valuable experience. At that time many prominent churchmen were opposed to the use of the organ or any type of musical instrument to accompany the voice, regarding such practice as worldly and wicked. For several years the choir director had to depend upon such precarious methods as the old tuning-fork or humming the scale to aid his singers in getting their parts. All of this undoubtedly increased the accuracy of his musical ear. However, it was eventually discovered that most of the church members favoured the purchase of an organ. The day of its introduction was a momentous one. Sankey himself presided at the instrument, and only one or two of the older members of the congregation left during the singing. During his years as choir leader of his own church Sankey often supplemented the musical program with personal solos, much to the delight of his listeners, and thus he was unconsciously preparing for the great work that should take him before thousands of audiences in this nation and in Europe.

In his position as class leader Sankey felt his responsibility in having the oversight of Christians older than himself, and was thus driven to careful study of the Bible. It was his custom to urge the members of his class to express their spiritual condition in language that was Scriptural. He also enriched his class meetings by occasional outbursts of song and thus maintained a full class. His charming voice was also an asset in his position as Sunday school superintendent, and he stressed the importance of gospel singing in the school.

When in the spring of 1860 President Lincoln called for men to sustain the government, Sankey was one of the first young men of his country to enrol as a soldier. His company was sent to Maryland. In the army his irrepressible love of singing endeared him to his companions, and he often led the singing for the religious services in the camp. He soon found other singers among his associates, and together they were invited out by families who enjoyed the singing of the "boys in blue." In later years Sankey recalled incidents when the boys would gather about the piano in those beautiful Southern homes, and any feeling of enmity would vanish under the spell of those songs so dear to the hearts of all Americans. At the expiration of his term of enlistment Sankey would have volunteered again, but was urged to return to Newcastle in order to assist his father who had been appointed by President Lincoln as a collector of internal revenue.

On the ninth of September, 1863, Sankey married Miss Fanny V. Edwards daughter of the Honourable John Edwards. Miss Edwards had been a member of his choir and a teacher in the Sunday school. Their union proved a happy one, and Mrs. Sankey became a cheerful, self-sacrificing companion to her evangelist husband. The Sankeys were the parents of three sons, one of whom was born in Scotland.

In 1867, when Sankey was twenty-seven years of age, a branch of the Young Men's Christian Association was organised at Newcastle, of which he first became secretary and later president. The group held its first meetings in a small rented room. Many years later, after Sankey had become a world-renowned gospel singer, he had the pleasure of presenting to his city a Young Men's Christian Association building, including a gymnasium and library, costing more than $40,000, with funds realised from the sale of his "Gospel Hymns". It was his association with the YMCA that was to be responsible for bringing the singer to the attention of the great Moody, a meeting which resulted in the formation of one of the greatest evangelistic teams of all times.

Sankey's fame as a singer spread throughout Western Pennsylvania and Eastern Ohio. The young man received invitation after invitation to sing for conventions, conferences, and political gatherings. Having a firm conviction that the Gospel should be sung as well as preached, he accepted these opportunities. It was his practice, however, never to receive any compensation for such services. It is thus seen that Sankey had no desire to practice singing as a profession. He made no effort to study music as an art. His gift of song was entirely consecrated to the cause of Christ, as were all his ransomed powers and that consecration was made a blessing to the multitudes.

In his work with the Young Men's Christian Association Sankey found an ever-widening field of usefulness. In June of 1870 he was sent as a delegate to an international convention of that group held in Indianapolis. For several years he had read with interest in the religious press of the work of Dwight L. Moody. It was with real pleasure, then, that he learned that Mr. Moody would be attending the convention as a representative of the Chicago Association. Little did he realise, however, that his meeting with Moody would prove the turning point of his career. For a few days Sankey met with disappointment, for he neither saw nor heard the famed Moody. At length his opportunity came. It was announced that Mr. Moody would be leading a six o'clock morning prayer meeting in the Baptist Church. Sankey arrived at the service a little late and sat near the door with a Presbyterian minister, a delegate from his own county, who informed him that the singing so far had been abominable and urged Sankey to start up a song. At the opportune moment the sweet singer began the strains of the familiar hymn, "There is a Fountain Filled with Blood." The congregation joined heartily, and the meeting took on a new impetus. At the close of the service Sankey's Presbyterian friend asked to introduce him to Mr. Moody. In a few terse queries Moody asked, "Where are you from? Are you married? What is your business?" Upon being informed that he was in the government's employ, the evangelist remarked abruptly, "You will have to give it up."

Sankey was nonplussed; then Moody declared, "I have been looking for you for eight years." At that moment the young man who had been singing the Gospel since childhood faced the most significant decision of his life.

Free From The Law, O Happy Condition

Free from the law, O happy condition
Jesus hath bled, and there is remission;
Cursed by the law and bruised by the fall,
Grace hath redeemed us once for all.

Once for all - O sinner receive it!
Once for all - O brother believe it!
Cling to the cross, the burden will fall;
Christ hath redeemed us once for all.

Now are we free - there's no condemnation;
Jesus provides a perfect salvation;
"Come unto Me", O hear His sweet call,
Come, and He saves us once for all.

Children of God, O glorious calling!
Surely His grace will keep us from falling;
Passing from death to life at His call,
Blessed salvation once for all.

2

"PROFITABLE TO ME FOR THE MINISTRY"
II Timothy 4:11

I f Ira D. Sankey's first meeting with his future colleague seemed romantic, the events of the next few days were none the less interesting. The singer had never seriously considered giving up his business, and was not yet ready to give Mr. Moody a pledge that he would sever his former relationships and join him in the evangelisation of the great city of Chicago. The preacher confided in his new-found friend that his chief problem in connection with his meetings was the singing. Since he was no singer himself, he had been compelled to rely upon all kinds of persons to lead his song services. Often when he was about to "pull the net" at the conclusion of his message, much effect of the service was lost through poor singing. Sankey was definitely interested, but not yet ready to render a decision. The following day Moody asked him to meet at a certain street corner. When the evangelist arrived, he made no explanations, but obtained a box from a store near by and asked Sankey to mount the box and sing something. The latter complied with "Am I a Soldier of the Cross." Moody then began to speak. A large crowd of men leaving the mills gathered to listen. After a few minutes, he announced that the meeting would continue at the Opera House. Sankey led the group, singing, "Shall We Gather at the River," and the large Opera House was packed in a few minutes. Sankey was further impressed, but not yet ready to enter the field of evangelism for life.

Six months later Sankey consented to spend a week with Mr. Moody in his work at Chicago. The two visited the sick, held noonday prayer meetings in the business districts, conducted services in the Illinois Street Church, and concluded with a great mass meeting in Farwell Hall. At this final service Sankey sang, "Come Home, O Prodigal Child." He then returned to his home, where he consulted with his pastor and friends, all of whom felt that his work was with Mr. Moody. Consequently his resignation was sent to the Secretary of the Treasury, and he launched forth upon a life of faith.

Sankey began his work with Moody early in 1871 and laboured with him daily until the church was destroyed in the great fire which swept Chicago that fall. It was Sunday evening, October 8, 1871. Mr. Moody had just finished speaking to an audience that crowded Farwell Hall to the doors. In compliance with his request, Mr. Sankey had stepped beside the great organ to sing. When he reached the verse,

"Today the Saviour calls:
For refuge fly;
The storm of justice falls,
And death is nigh,"

his voice was drowned by the clanging of fire engines as they rushed past the hall and the tolling of bells in the general alarm. Confusion rose from the streets, and Moody decided to dismiss the congregation which was becoming restless. He and his co-worker left by a small stairway and for a few moments watched the reflection of the fire that was then raging on the west side of the city. The two men parted, not to meet again for two months.

Sankey often had occasion to recall the events of that memorable night. At first he hastened to the scene of the fire and aided in trying to prevent the spread of the conflagration. A wind of almost hurricane proportions swept in from the southwest, and it was evident that the city was doomed. All the time the fire was moving toward the business section and Farwell Hall. Sankey hastened to his rooms in the Farwell Hall building, with the flames following so closely that he was compelled to shake the falling embers from his coat. Arriving at his room, he grabbed his most valued possessions and left the building. He sought some means of conveyance in vain, and finally started toward Lake Michigan, carrying his belongings. After many harrowing experiences, he reached the lake shore in safety, but exhausted and very thirsty. By this time the city water works and gasworks had been destroyed. Almost desperate for water, Sankey found a small rowboat and, rolling his possessions on board, rowed out far enough to find fresh water. Tying his boat in position, he watched the destruction of that great city. Night had passed and now the sun of October 9th had sunk in the West, but the city was still wrapped in flames. At that juncture Sankey determined to return to shore but discovered to his dismay that the line which fastened his boat had broken. He was swept out on the rolling lake, and for the moment his life was endangered. But Providence overruled, and he returned to land.

It seemed that the great work of Moody and Sankey in the Windy City had ended. The latter telegraphed his family of his safety and took an outgoing train for his Pennsylvania home. Two months lapsed before he was to learn of the welfare of his friend and co-labourer. Undoubtedly those were days of severe trial of his faith. But eventually a brief telegram from Moody invited him to return to Chicago to assist in the rude temporary tabernacle that had been constructed. Speaking later of the great fire, Moody remarked, "All I saved was my Bible, my family and my reputation."

The two consecrated men continued to minister to the poor and needy who had lost everything. They slept together in a corner of the tabernacle with only a single lounge for a bed. When the wild prairie winds blew, snow often drifted into the room. But they laboured on, visiting and supplying the needs of the destitute by day and ministering to their spiritual needs in the great tabernacle every night. During these busy months Moody was soliciting funds from his friends for the reconstruction of the church. In his characteristic manner he overcame all obstacles, and the new edifice far exceeded the one that had been reduced to ashes.

Mr. Sankey moved his family to Chicago in October 1872. It was in this year that Moody made a second evangelistic trip to England, leaving the great work in Chicago in the hands of Sankey, who was ably assisted by such men as Major Whittle, Fleming H. Revell, and Richard Thain. During this time Sankey was also devoting much time to the selection of such hymns and spiritual songs as would best suit his evangelistic work. He was fortunate in having several contemporaries who were devoting themselves seriously to the task of producing beautiful spiritual lyrics and lively revival tunes. Often Sankey composed his tunes, for these seemed best suited to the spirit of the singer and to the rich quality of his baritone voice. Upon Moody's return from England, he discovered that his friend had imbibed much of that increased evangelistic passion which he had felt abroad. The two worked together, in a spirit of beautiful harmony as becomes well-chosen counterparts, to the reviving of many churches and scores of individual Christians.

An evangelistic campaign in Springfield, Illinois was attended with unusual power and blessing. Indeed if the evangelists had remained in their own country at that time, there was every promise of a gracious revival. However, God was leading unmistakably, and His two servants were ready to do His bidding.

About this time Sankey's esteemed friend Philip Phillips had returned from Europe where he had been singing for one hundred successive nights. He now had an impressive engagement on the Pacific coat. He met Sankey and made him an enticing offer, including a handsome salary and all expenses to accompany him and assist in his services of song.

A man of superficial consecration would no doubt have been swayed by the proposal, but Sankey's life was not his own. After several hours of prayer and consultation with Mr. Moody, he declined and determined to continue his life of faith in the ministry of evangelistic singing.

Had Moody entertained a doubt as to the wisdom of his partnership with the gifted singer of Methodism, he had long ago had ample proof of the success of that alliance. In the words of the great Apostle he could gratefully acknowledge that Sankey "was profitable to me for the Gospel." In every respect the singer was the counterpart of the preacher. Moody succeeded because of his earnestness, without the grace of voice or manner. Sankey possessed grace of both voice and manner and natural culture which endeared him to all. Lacking the physical and mental force of his fellow-labourer, Sankey had a most pleasing personal appearance. His countenance was open, genial and expressive and often while he sang, it glowed with an inner blessing and radiance. The effect of Moody's sermons was to arouse and startle his hearers; Sankey's songs tended to soothe and comfort. At the conclusion of one of the evangelist's soul-stirring appeals, Sankey would arise and sing, with the conviction that souls were accepting Christ between one note and the next. It could never be fully determined who drew the greater crowds to the large tabernacles, the preacher or his singer. At any rate, Moody determined to take his associate with him on his next trip abroad.

There Were Ninety And Nine

There were ninety and nine that safely lay
In the shelter of the fold;
But one was out on the hills away,
Far off from the gates of gold,
Away on the mountains wild and bare,
Away from the tender Shepherd's care.

Lord, Thou hast here Thy ninety and nine,
Are they not enough for Thee?
But the Shepherd made answer:
This of Mine
Has wandered away from Me;
And although the road be rough and steep,
I go to the desert to find My sheep.

But none of the ransomed ever knew
How deep were the waters crossed;
Nor how dark was the night that the Lord passed through
Ere He found His sheep that was lost:
Out in the desert He heard its cry,
Sick and helpless and ready to die.

over/

Lord, whence are those blood-drops all the way,
That mark out the mountain's track?
They were shed for one who had gone astray
Ere the Shepherd could bring him back.
Lord, whence are Thy hands so rent and torn?
They are pierced tonight by many a thorn.

But all through the mountains thunder-riven
And up from the rocky steep,
There arose a cry to the gates of heaven:
Rejoice! I have found My sheep!
And the angels echoed around the throne,
Rejoice! for the Lord brings back His own!

3

"LISTEN, O ISLES"
Isaiah 49:1

<hr>

The remarkable evangelistic tour through Great Britain which resulted in a tremendous spiritual awakening, the impact of which was felt throughout Christendom, was undertaken by Moody and Sankey in 1837. In June of that year they sailed, Mr. Moody accompanied by his family, and Mr. Sankey by his wife. Sankey proved a good seaman, whereas his associate spent the greater part of the voyage in his berth. The trip was otherwise uneventful. When the vessel stopped at Queensland to receive mail, Mr. Moody received the perplexing news that both the men who had extended him the invitation to England were dead. It looked for a moment as if God was closing the door. The party landed in Liverpool, without an invitation, without a committee to welcome them, and with very little money.

Again they were called upon to exercise a greater dependence upon God.

Looking over some mail he had received in New York which was yet unread, Mr. Moody found a letter from the secretary of the Young Men's Christian Association at York, inviting the evangelist to speak there if he should ever visit England again. Accepting his partly-open door, the two men proceeded to York, where they were received with much surprise and not too much enthusiasm. However, the secretary obtained the use of the Independent Chapel, and evangelistic services were announced. The first service was attended by fewer than fifty persons, and Mr. Sankey's first song service in England could not be called successful, for the people were unaccustomed to his methods and to the type of songs he used. The first noonday prayer meeting was attended by only six persons but the two courageous warriors were undaunted. A few days later the pastor of the leading Baptist church of the city arose in one of these meetings and testified to the truth of Mr. Moody's preaching on the necessity of the Holy Spirit for service. For two days he had been closeted in prayer and had returned to the service to witness to the new experience he had received. This testimony proved the beginning of a gracious spiritual revival. Within a few days hundreds were crowding the inquiry room. That young pastor whose confession and subsequent ministry brought blessing to uncounted thousands was none other than the famous Rev. F. B. Meyer.

By this time invitations were pouring in from various towns in the vicinity, and Moody and Sankey began their labours with Reverent Rees at Sunderland. Not aware of the pastor's opposition to solo singing, as well as to organs and choirs, Mr. Sankey sang several of his favourite songs. The pastor was definitely impressed. Within a few days he posted notices announcing that Mr. Sankey of Chicago would "sing the gospel." It is interesting to note that his phrase was originated by one of the most conservative ministers in all England. A small cabinet organ was brought into the chapel and given a conspicuous place from which Mr. Sankey could lead the singing.

One night at Sunderland at the conclusion of an earnest message Mr. Sankey was requested to sing "Come Home, O Prodigal, Come Home." A hush prevailed as his voice in pathos carried the plea to his hearers. Suddenly a cry pierced the silence, and a young man rushed forward and fell in the arms of his father, begging forgiveness. His father assured him of his forgiveness and, in turn, led him to the inquiry room where both might seek the forgiveness of God. The entire congregation was profoundly impressed, and hundreds pressed to the adjoining room, seeking prayer and pardon. Conviction deepened throughout the city; the largest hall was engaged for the remainder of the services and crowded to the door at each service.

Receiving a petition from Newcastle which was signed by a large number of non-conformist ministers and a few prominent laymen, Mr. Moody and his associate moved on to that city. Prospects were not so promising the first night, for only a few were present, but within a few days the chapel was so crowded that overflow meeting had to be held in neighbouring halls. At this place the Quakers or Friends became greatly interested in the services, and were especially attracted to the songs of Sankey which were new to them. It was at this place that he first began using the songs, "The Sweet By and By," "That will be Heaven for Me," and "Christ Arose." With surprising animation the people took up these songs and soon they could be heard in the shipyards and in the market places, on the streets and in the railway trains. It was at Newcastle also that the first great "Moody and Sankey" choir was organised. Revival fires continued to burn in Newcastle for two months, at times with such fervor that as many as thirty-four meetings were held in a single week.

While still engaged at Newcastle, the evangelists were met by a refined Scotch gentleman who asked whether they would consider going to Scotland upon invitation from the ministers there. This man had been attending the meetings for ten days and had been reporting to his ministerial friends in Scotland. As a result of this interview the invitation to minister in Scotland was accepted. However, a series of meetings was first held in the border town of Carlisle. For a few days the services lacked power. Upon inquiry Mr. Moody learned that the ministers of the place were accusing him of "sheep stealing". The evangelist informed his accusers that this was the first time he had ever met with such an accusation and that he never worked in the interest of building up or tearing down any denomination. He then requested each of those present to lead in prayer. The result was a kindly and brotherly spirit which prevailed throughout the gracious services that followed.

It was to Scotland that the singer proceeded with some misgivings and with no small degree of anxiety. There was much prejudice against the singing of so-called "human" hymns as any song apart from the Psalms was called, and animosity toward the "kist o'whistles", as the type of cabinet organ that Mr. Sankey used was termed even greater. The first meeting in Edinburgh was scheduled for Sunday night, November 23. As if to add to the singer's burden, Mr. Moody had contracted a severe cold and was unable to speak. Rev. J. H. Wilson was to take his place. Long before the hour of service the large Music Hall was packed to its capacity, with other thousands seeking admittance. Exercising his great tactfulness, Mr. Sankey first invited the congregation to join in singing a portion of the One Hundredth Psalm. This they did with a will, and Scripture reading and prayer followed. Sankey was now faced with the serious innovation of singing the gospel, a matter which had been much discussed throughout Scotland. The number selected for his first solo was "Jesus of Nazareth Passeth By." With a prayer on his heart and infinite tenderness in his voice, the singer was soon conscious of an intense silence over the audience which bore mute testimony that his hearers were accepting this novel method of presenting the gospel story. After the message his solo was "Hold the Fort". He asked the congregation to join in the chorus. They complied with such celerity and power that Sankey was thoroughly convinced that gospel songs would prove as effective in reaching the masses in Scotland as they had in America and in England.

A few nights later Sankey's faith in the power of song was still more deeply tried. Upon his arrival at the organ he discovered that Dr. Horatius Bonar was seated close by. That prince among hymnists, whose opinions Sankey valued more than any man's in Scotland, would not sing his own beautiful hymns because he ministered in a church that believed only in using the Psalms. With much trepidation Sankey announced his solo, "Free from the Law, Oh Happy Condition". He then bowed his head and offered a fervent prayer which relieved his anxiety. At the close of that service Dr. Bonar greeted him with a smile and with the gracious remark, "Well, Mr. Sankey, you sang the gospel tonight."

The innovation of gospel singing and the organ in Scotland gave rise to several amusing incidents. One night in the Edinburgh meeting in the Free Assembly Hall, Mr. Sankey began to sing his solo, when a shrill voice was heard in the gallery as a woman made her way to the door, shouting, "Let me oot! Let me oot! What would John Knox think of the like of you?" The solo ended, Mr. Sankey made his way to the church across the street where a great overflow crowd had assembled. No sooner had be begun singing than the same voice begged, "Let me oot! Let me oot! What would John Knox think of the like of you?"

In the North of Scotland, where it was feared Sankey's singing would meet with the deepest prejudice, his songs evoked special favour and soon the shepherds on the hillsides were singing his melodies as they tended their sheep. These sweet gospel refrains soon came to express the feelings of the lords and ladies of the castles and the lowly errand boys of the streets. Everywhere Sankey was able to sing his way into the hearts of the people with such persuasiveness that those who came to criticise returned with their prejudice broken and their hearts unmistakeably impressed. It was not long until he was acclaimed the most popular sacred singer of the United Kingdom.

In Edinburgh the revival services were attended by ministers of all denominations from all parts of the country. There were also distinguished members of the nobility, professors from the University, and lawyers from the Parliament House present to listen to the ministry in sermon and in song. The evangelistic campaign continued in Great Britain for two years, with ever-widening influence and power.

Remarkable incidents, too numerous for earth's record attended the great revival campaigns throughout the British Isles. God had commanded, "Listen, O Isles" and multitudes had listened to the salvation of their souls. The voices of preacher and singer would never be forgotten by those who heard. The campaign had been long and strenuous and Moody and his colleague felt that the time had come to return to their native land.

Pass Me Not, O Gentle Saviour

Pass me not, O gentle Saviour,
Hear my humble cry;
While on others Thou art calling,
Do not pass me by.

Saviour! Saviour!
Hear my humble cry,
While on others Thou art calling,
Do not pass me by.

Let me at Thy throne of mercy
Find a sweet relief;
Kneeling there in deep contrition,
Help my unbelief.

Trusting only in Thy merit,
Would I seek Thy face;
Heal my wounded, broken spirit,
Save me by Thy grace.

Thou the spring of all my comfort,
More than life to me,
Whom have I on earth beside Thee?
Whom in heaven but Thee?

4

"IN HIS OWN COUNTRY"
Matthew 13:57

After their memorable farewell at Liverpool, Moody and Sankey proceeded to the ship, the "Spain", upon which they had secured their homeward passage. Several thousands, applauding loudly and singing many of the favourite gospel hymns, accompanied them to the pier. During the voyage to America the passengers were blessed by the songs of Sankey. When questioned relative to their phenomenal success in Great Britain, the two men would humbly remark, "God was in it."

Arriving in New York on August 14th, 1875, the evangelists felt the need of rest and reunion with loved ones from whom they had been so long separated. But almost immediately they were visited by delegations desiring their services in many important cities of the nation. At Northfield, Massachusetts, Moody's home town, the first service of the now-famed evangelistic team was marked by a singular event. Moody's mother, a Unitarian, stood up for prayer. It was in this service also that Sankey sang, "The Ninety and Nine" for the first time in America.

Progressive Christians in Brooklyn, New York, began making extensive preparations to invite the evangelists to their city. The first service was held in the Clermont Avenue Rink which had been secured for that purpose. Although the service was announced for eight-thirty in the morning, the great auditorium was packet to its capacity long before the hour, and thousands were turned away for want of room. Throngs also crowded the Talmage Tabernacle for morning prayer services. In the services at the Rink Mr. Sankey was assisted by a great choir of two hundred and fifty voices. A large organ assisted the choir and audience, but Mr. Sankey accompanied his solos on a small organ, a practice which he always preferred. at no time would he allow the music to detract from the message of his song. From the opening service to the final benediction a month later the revival in Brooklyn was a grand triumph. It was estimated that twenty thousand persons heard the gospel in song and sermon daily and that as many as three thousand attended the inquiry meetings. It was at one of the latter that Mr. Sankey was instrumental in leading an avowed infidel, a fine young engineer, to Christ.

Chief among the earnest men in Philadelphia making preparation for the coming of the Moody-Sankey party to their city was John Wanamaker. It was he who had the old Pennsylvania Railroad Depot converted into an auditorium seating more than ten thousand persons at a cost of twenty thousand dollars. Expectation ran high as the date for opening, November 21, drew near. Day dawned, with the rain coming down in torrents. Churches were practically deserted for the day, but at least nine thousand people assembled at the Market Street Tabernacle for the opening service there. At the close of a stirring appeal by the evangelist, Sankey sang,

> *"Hark the voice of Jesus crying,*
> *Who will go and work today?"*

in a manner such as the Quaker City had never heard before. From the beginning of the campaign Sankey was assisted by a choir of no less than five hundred voices who had trained prior to his arrival. Thanksgiving Day was celebrated at the Tabernacle in an unforgettable manner. Sankey's singing of "The Ninety and Nine" was a highlight of the day. One once occasion President Grant, several senators and members of the Supreme Court attended the Philadelphia meeting. When the regular revival services ended on January 16, religious interest in the city was still deepening. It was believed that the meetings had a total attendance of seven hundred thousand. The unanimous testimony of those who had prepared for the revival was that it had far outreached their highest hopes.

A number of Princeton students, who attended the Philadelphia meetings, invited Moody and Sankey to conduct services at the College, an invitation which was readily accepted. The revival at Princeton was one of the most remarkable that the school ever experienced.

On the site of the present Madison Square Garden the old Hippodrome, always a place of sport and gaiety, was converted into a vast assembly hall, where Mr. Moody and his compeer were greeted by the largest audiences that had up to that date convened in the metropolis. A choir of six hundred voices sang the great hymns that characterised the Moody-Sankey revivals.

The New York campaign, conducted in the early spring of 1876, lasted ten weeks and resulted in the conversion of several thousand persons.

His health having been somewhat impaired Mr. Sankey returned to his home in Newcastle for a brief respite, but even then he was busy in the preparation of his song book, "Gospel Hymns Number Two", in which he was assisted by his esteemed friend Mr. P. P. Bliss. Then he was called by his co-labourer to Chicago where the two held forth for three months in a large tabernacle especially constructed for the purpose. It was here that the singer was called to mourn the untimely death of Mr. and Mrs. Bliss with whom he had long been associated in the ministry of song. The train which was to have carried them to Chicago wrecked, and the beloved hymn writer and his wife were among the victims of that disaster. At the close of the Chicago mission a farewell service was conducted for those who had been brought to Christ during the campaign. This service was attended by six thousand persons.

Of singular interest was the evangelistic campaign conducted in Boston, the hub of American culture and a city noted for its knowledge and love of music. Would the simple melodies of Sankey and his unartistic manner of singing them satisfy the public interest? No doubt the desire to hear him sing was as great as the desire to listen to famous co-labourer? In the opening service, held January 28, 1877, in a great temporary structure erected for the revival, the singer, who had charmed multitudes both in the Old World and the New, was seated humbly at his small organ. When the familiar "There Were Ninety and Nine" was announced, he arose and offered an earnest prayer for the success of his message in song. Then as the sweet strains of song filled the auditorium, his listeners were enchained with his power to touch the secret chords of the human heart, and his success in the staid old city was assured. At Boston an average of three services were held daily, and the evangelists enjoyed the fellowship of many noted divines, among whom were the Dr. A. J. Gordon, Dr. Joseph Cook and Phillips Brooks. Several other campaigns were conducted in the New England area.

The revival work of Moody and Sankey was not confined to the East and Middle West, for calls came from hundreds of cities across the nation. Meetings were also held in Canada and in Mexico and were marked by the same success as that enjoyed in the United States. The next several years were punctuated by several trips to Great Britain. One of the great joys of these campaigns was to meet with converts of former years. In the series of 1881-84 services were conducted in ninety-nine cities and towns of Scotland alone.

In commenting upon their success abroad one prominent Englishman remarked, "These American laymen ... have probably left a deeper impress of their individuality upon the men and women of Great Britain than any other persons that could be named."

Mr. Sankey's keen sense of humour is shown by a single incident that took place one time on the train between Chicago and New York. A gentleman seated beside him entered into a conversation which eventually drifted to the subject of religion. The stranger said that he had never had the pleasure of meeting Moody or Sankey. His companion assured that he had often heard both. When asked what kind of persons they were, Sankey replied, "Oh they are just common folks like you and me."

The stranger continued that his danger had a cabinet organ and that they were all fond of the "Gospel Hymns". He then expressed regret that he had not heard Sankey sing "The Ninety and Nine" before the famed singer's death. Sankey expressed surprise, but his companion affirmed that he had read the news of Sankey's death in the papers. As they neared the station where his friend was to leave the train, Sankey felt that it was fair to reveal his identity. To the inquiry, "Who are you?" he replied, "I am what is left of Sankey".

The associations of Sankey with Moody continued for nearly a quarter of a century. In addition to his faithful singing of the gospel, a feature which undoubtedly was of inestimable worth in popularising the great revival campaigns, Sankey gave active support to Moody's educational ventures. The result was the famous schools at Northfield and Mount Herman. The two men agreed to utilise the royalty received from their hymn books in establishing the first of these institutions, a school designed for the education of underprivileged girls in New England. A little later a boy's school was founded and thousands of young men and woman who might never have enjoyed the advantages of a good education became useful citizens because of the far reaching vision of Moody and Sankey.

The final evangelistic service of the famous pair was held in the church of Dr. Storr in Brooklyn. Mr. Sankey later recalled that the evangelist seemed to have just as much power and unction upon him as he had ever witnessed in all their years of united labours. The hearts of all present seemed to be strangely moved, and hundreds tarried after the service to recall the blessed memories of the great campaign held in their city just twenty-five years before. A few weeks later the two spent a Sunday together in New York and then parted for the last time. Mr. Sankey received a letter from Moody dated November 6th, 1899, which was to be his last. It contained nine pages in which the great man spoke with fervour of his work in Northfield and Chicago. Sankey held high hopes of meeting him again, but just a little later, December 22nd, Moody's forty-four years of consecrated service were terminated at Kansas City, when soon after he literally "died in harness". Thus death dissolved one of the most effective gospel teams of all times.

Having sung his way into the hearts of millions in his own country, as well as abroad, Sankey continued conducting services of "Sacred Song and Story" for some time.

"Almost Persuaded"

"Almost persuaded" now to believe;
"Almost persuaded" Christ to receive;
Seems now some soul to say:
Go, Spirit, go Thy way;
Some more convenient day
On Thee I'll call.

"Almost persuaded," come, come today!
"Almost persuaded," turn not away;
Jesus invites you here;
Angels are lingering near;
Prayers rise from hearts so dear;
O wanderer, come!

"Almost persuaded": harvest is past!
"Almost persuaded": doom comes at last;
"Almost" cannot avail;
"Almost is but to fail;
Sad, sad, that bitter wail:
"Almost" - but lost!

5

"ONE THAT HATH A PLEASANT VOICE"
Ezekiel 33:32

T he influence of music upon the hearts of men has been recognised in all ages. Battle-hymns of the nations have aroused the masses when words of the orator were futile. When all other arts failed, music brought back the reason of a distracted King Saul. Since music has such tremendous power, it is not surprising that servants of God in every age have employed it in propagating the religion which they sought to extol. Indeed the singing of songs was a statute to Israel. The disciples of Christ sang a hymn at the Last Supper, and Paul and Silas expressed themselves in song during their memorable imprisonment at Philippi. Church leaders of the early ages recognised the power of song, and the mighty Luther gave music a place of honour second only to theology. During the great revivals under the

Wesleys and Whitefield sacred music played a conspicuous part.

It seems fortunate, therefore, that Dwight L. Moody choose as his travelling companion and co-worker in the gospel a man whose silver tones had the power of conveying truth to the hearts of his hearers with a conviction that could not be shaken off. In every instance Mr. Sankey made his music subservient to the words, which he enunciated with the utmost clearness. His chief concern was to lead men to a definite surrender to Christ. At no time did he permit himself to be motivated by a desire for self display or for mere gratification of his hearers' curiosity. In all these respects every gospel singer of the twentieth century would do well to emulate his worthy example.

Innumerable instances could be cited to show the influence of Sankey's songs upon those who were privileged to hear him. On one occasion in Edinburgh a thoughtless young girl, unable to get into the building, remained outside. But the affectionate strains of "I Am so Glad that Jesus Loves Me" reached her where she was. Immediately she was touched and at the close of the service was an inquirer and a happy finder of salvation. In the same city a poor sin-laden man lingered a few minutes after the service, while the singer and his choir was practising.

> "Free from the law, oh, happy condition!
> Jesus hath bled, and there is remission."

The man surrendered his load of guilt and then and there found forgiveness.

It has been said that many of the most thrilling and marked cases of conversion in Scotland can be traced to the solos of Sankey. One notable case was that of an infidel who was zealously engaged in attacking Christianity. He came to the meetings to scoff and to expose the "humbug". One night Mr. Sankey sang that tender hymn, "Waiting and Watching for Me," with the exquisite sympathy that attended his solos. The infidel was reminded of the infant who had left him years ago. His heart was melted; he became an earnest Christian worker and one of Moody's best friends.

Another incident from Scotland is that of a well-known citizen, prominent in political circles, yet dissipated in life He was present at one of the services when Sankey sang, "Jesus of Nazareth Passeth By." The man had cherished a secret intention of one day becoming a Christian. But the last strain of the singer,

"Jesus of Nazareth hath passed by,"

awakened him to the terrible thought that Jesus might have passed him by. He hurried to his home where, on his knees pleading for mercy, he found peace in believing. Testimonies of this nature ran into hundreds, all proving the marvellous power of sacred song to lead men to salvation.

Christians were greatly encouraged to activity by Sankey's singing. When his magnetic voice rang out in earnest supplication or fervent praise, it seemed as if the whole audience would rise and join him in the grand musical prayer or thanksgiving, so great was his power to move men. Many hearty responses of "Amen" and "Glory to God" could be heard over the vast audiences, and men as well as women were melted to tears. There was a simplicity about his singing that had a way of disarming his severest critic. His voice had a charm all its own which attracted and held his hearers with a power that was gentle yet irresistible. Often upon hearing him sing, men would exclaim. "That is the most eloquent sermon I ever heard." His voice possessed a singular sweetness, flexibility and strength. Without the aid of modern knowledge of acoustics or public address systems, he was able to make himself heard distinctly by great audiences of ten to twenty thousand persons.

Not only was Mr. Sankey a singer of unusual merit himself, but he was able to inspire song in others. Rousing congregational singing was an important feature of the Moody-Sankey campaigns. Sankey was fortunate in living at an age of great composers of spiritual songs. It was his privilege to popularise scores of these songs until they could be heard throughout the civilised world and in foreign mission fields. The whistling or humming of Sankey's tunes was a favourite diversion of the working man. In their homes mothers sang their babies to sleep or performed their household tasks to the tunes learned at the Moody-Sankey revivals. Long after the words of the preacher were forgotten, the songs of the sweet singer lived on. Many of the songs that he introduced are favourites in Sunday Schools and churches yet today.

Sankey had definite ideas with respect to song leading and choir conducting which he attempted to put into practice whenever it was feasible. Song directors today would do well to inculcate some of his ideas and methods into their work. He believed that the church music should be conducted by a good choir of Christian singers who should encourage the congregation to sing rather than monopolise the service themselves. He wanted the singers and organ at the front of the church and as near the minister as possible for he felt they should cooperate fully with him throughout the service. He insisted on exemplary deportment on the part of choir members. He felt that all choir members should be Christians and that the director should be a Christian of influence. If he could not find sufficient members for the choir, he would go into the Sunday school and find them there.

While Mr. Sankey admired the large organ, he felt that people did not sing so well with it. Its loud tones, he believed, drowned the voices and people tended just to sit and listen without singing. For that reason he favoured the use of a small organ, especially in his solo work. He always insisted that the organist play softly, for it was the singing and not the music which he sought to emphasise in all his services. For that reason he felt that instrumental music, other than that necessary to keep the correct key, was not essential in the house of God.

At times Sankey would remark kindly that he did not feel that most ministers were as interested as they should be in the song service. He thought that the singing should be prayed for as much as the preaching, and he made it a practice to offer up an earnest petition when he rose to sing a solo, particularly if it was one of a serious nature designed to awaken the sinner. No doubt much of his own success in singing the gospel may be traced to the fact that his songs were well bathed in fervent prayer.

Mr. Sankey believed that the chorister should attend the Sunday school and prayer meetings. In that way only could he exert the right Christian influence upon his choir members. He encouraged such directors to open and close their practice sessions with prayer. In that way he felt that the group could be kept spiritual, for it was his opinion that at least four-fifths of the traditional trouble arising in choirs was caused by the ungodly element that got into them.

Aware of the fact that many people miss the message of song because of poor reading, Sankey often read the lines of a hymn to his congregation to insure their getting the proper interpretation and spirit. He also believed in taking time to tell the people just how he wanted them to sing a song. Such instructions were amply rewarded by better and more understandable singing on the part of his congregation. His own pronunciation was perfect and his enunciation clear. At times he interspersed the song service with an interesting anecdote. These were never told merely to take up time, but always with a purpose so that the song service became a vital force in creating the proper spiritual atmosphere in which the evangelist should preach.

It cannot be denied that Mr. Sankey considered his gospel singing a divine calling and not a mere profession. Often he was unable to determine what song should be used as Mr. Moody "drew the net" until the sermon was delivered.

Then he sang with great power and effectiveness. On many occasions Mr. Moody would request a certain song. His co-worker showed a spirit of genuine helpfulness by graciously complying.

Whatever else may be said in praise of the sweet singer of Methodism, utter simplicity was one of the most definite indications of his true greatness. At no time would be guilty of doing anything for mere effect. His hearers were certain of the whole-hearted earnestness of his appeal. Perhaps that is the reason many of the same songs which he made famous when sung by some so-called gospel singers today are rendered meaningless and flat. It could be said of Sankey that he sang "with the spirit and with the understanding also". Hence he was able to move others and to quicken their understanding of the glorious gospel that he sang.

The songs of Sankey did much to revolutionise church music, particularly in the British Isles where churches had for the most part drifted into a deadly formalism. In America, too, his work gave impetus to church singing and pioneered the way for a succession of divinely-called evangelistic singers, who devote their entire time to singing the gospel.

In other words of scripture, Sankey was "One that had a pleasant voice," and it pleased God to take that voice, completely dedicated to His glory, and use it to bring blessing and salvation to the multitudes.

The Lord's Our Rock

The Lord's our Rock, in Him we hide,
  A shelter in the time of storm;
    Secure whatever ill betide,
  A shelter in the time of storm.

O Jesus is a Rock in a weary land,
  A weary land, a weary land;
O Jesus is a Rock in a weary land,
  A shelter in the time of storm.

A shade by day, defence by night,
  A shelter in the time of storm;
No fears alarm, no foes affright,
  A shelter in the time of storm.

The raging storms may round us beat,
  A shelter in the time of storm;
We'll never leave our safe retreat,
  A shelter in the time of storm.

O Rock divine, O Refuge dear,
  A shelter in the time of storm;
Be Thou our Helper, ever near,
  A shelter in the time of storm.

6

"SINGING AND MAKING MELODY"
Ephesians 5:19

O ne cannot doubt that Sankey's life was in his music. He achieved undying fame not only as a gospel singer, but as a composer of sacred tunes. This talent began to show itself early, for at the age of fifteen he began to compose tunes for his own amusement. Later his gospel hymns were to encircle the globe and to be sung in many languages. All of his tunes were essentially improvisations, some of them being composed as the occasion demanded. His famous hymn "The Ninety and Nine" was composed in this manner.

The word of the song, written by Elizabeth Clephane, came to Sankey's attention in a providential way. As he was leaving Glasgow, Scotland, he picked up a newspaper in a

railway coach, in hopes of finding some news from America.
In that quest he was disappointed, but his eyes suddenly
lighted upon a poem that impressed him deeply. He cut it
out and placed it in his musical scrapbook. Some time later
Mr. Moody and others were speaking upon the subject "The
Good Shepherd". The evangelist turned to his singer and
asked for a solo appropriate to the subject. Sankey was seized
with a sudden impression to sing the beautiful words he had
found a few days before. Hesitating only a moment, he placed
the newspaper clipping on the organ, and lifting his heart in
fervent prayer for aid, struck the key A flat and began to
sing in unforgettable tones,

"There were ninety and nine that safely lay."

Note by note the tune was given to him to the very last strain.
At the conclusion, Moody declared that he had never heard
anything like it in his life. One cannot doubt that God gave
the beloved singer the tune that was to sing its way into the
hearts of multitudes throughout the world. Many have testified definitely to being led to the Shepherd's fold through
the power of that hymn.

While Mr. Sankey was able to sing the grand old hymns
of the church with great power, his greatest triumphs were
the music of his own creation. Nevertheless, some of the
most popular and effective of his solos were the songs of
Mr. Bliss. Sankey's tunes were characterised by a greater
freedom and more popular appeal than early church music.
His melodies had a variety and lightness which sometimes
shocked his more conservative hearers.

Although Mr. Moody was not a singer and evidently possessed no ear for music at all, Sankey always respected his judgment in the preparation of hymn tunes. He attributed much of his inspiration for composing music to Moody and felt assured that if his tune impressed his older associate it would also appeal to the public. Almost without fail Moody's impressions were right. It seems that this man of God possessed an almost uncanny sense of discerning what would touch the hearts of men. Sankey, no doubt, profited by taking the counsel of Moody.

Admirers and critics alike agree upon one point: that Sankey was able to move humanity by the power of music as few men have ever done. A music critic, not especially in sympathy with the evangelist's religious efforts, commenting in one of the musical journals of London at the time of the Moody-Sankey revival there, asserted that Sankey's music had a grandeur greater than that of a Handel Festival, different in its grandeur, to be sure, but more impressive because it was natural, spontaneous and enthusiastic. It seems likely that no opera tenor, no successful actor, nor any platform orator ever had more enthusiastic audiences or received more lavish flattery than did Sankey. Yet he maintained an inherent humility, for he recognised his gifts as from God and refused to allow earthly acclaim to swerve him from his sole purpose in life - to win men to the Christ.

From an inauspicious beginning in England in 1873 the publishing interests of Sankey grew to tremendous proportions. That first book, really a tiny pamphlet containing twenty-three pieces and called "Sacred Songs and Solos," paved the way for the "Gospel Hymns" numbers one through six which were prepared and published from 1875 to 1891 and contained hundreds of hymns that are still widely used. In much of this work Sankey was assisted by several able hymn writers. In some instances he composed the tunes himself.

Royalties from his song books would have brought Sankey and his family a modest fortune. However, from the beginning he realised no personal profit from this work, having decided to devote such funds to the cause of Christian education.

Mr. Sankey was also interested in the history of hymns and through the years collected interesting data on their composition. To this he added a wealth of incidents which illustrated the success that he, as well as other evangelists, had had in using these songs. When the manuscript, which he planned to publish, was almost complete, it was destroyed in 1901 by the fires which swept the large Sanatorium in Battle Creek, Michigan where Sankey was a guest of Dr. J. H. Kellogg. In order not to disappoint his friends who were wanting such a book the courageous man undertook the stupendous task of rewriting as much of it as possible from memory. The result was the publication of "My Life and the Story of Gospel Hymns" in 1906. In this work Mr. Sankey has made a valuable contribution in the field of hymnology.

Among the cherished friends of Mr. Sankey was Fanny J. Crosby, the blind poetess and writer of sacred songs and hymns. For several years this esteemed lady spent her summers with the Sankeys at Northfield. On one occasion in 1886 Sankey had composed a tune for which he asked Miss Crosby to write a poem. She declined for the moment, but in a surprisingly short time, as she sat at the piano, the following words came to her,

> *"O child of God, wait patiently*
> *When dark thy path may be, etc."*

Many disheartened souls have found comfort in this hymn.

Two of the most familiar and affective invitation hymns made popular by the Moody-Sankey campaigns are "Pass me Not" and "Almost Persuaded". The former, a hymn of Fanny Crosby, was a great favourite in the London revival and many were moved to a decision for Christ by its stirring appeal. The latter, a work of Mr. Bliss, was sung very effectively by Sankey. Many have witnessed to having yielded under its warning; some testified to having rejected mercy while the hymn was sung, and died with the final strains ringing in their ears. Other songs of this type, for which Sankey himself provided the tunes and which proved very useful, were "Why Not Tonight?", "Yet There Is Room", "Welcome, Wanderer, Welcome", "Take Me As I Am", and "I Am Praying For You". The fact that these songs are still widely used in revival work is evidence of the effectual message contained in their words and music.

Among the best known songs designed to bring courage and comfort to the Christian, for which Sankey composed the music and which he used successfully in his work, are "A Shelter in the Time of Storm," "Hiding in Thee," "It is Finished," "Jesus, I Will Trust Thee," "Not Now, My Child," "Tell It Out," "Beneath the Cross of Jesus," "The Smitten Rock," "There'll be no Dark Valley," "Trusting Jesus, That is All," "Under His Wing," and "When the Mists Have Rolled Away." Nearly all of these are still favourites among Christians everywhere.

Sankey was ever alert to find new poems which could be set to music. His resourcefulness is shown in his ability to choose sacred songs of almost every type and suitable to all occasions. A reading of the titles of his songs indicate that they run the entire gamut of human emotions and human experience. This fact assures such songs an enduring ministry in the Christian church. The heritage of sacred music which the now sainted Sankey left us is immeasurably rich and precious.

Only a few times did Sankey attempt to write both the words and music for a song. The last of such efforts was made upon the occasion of Mr. Moody's death, and the song was entitled "Out of the Shadow-land". Sankey sang the song as a solo in the great memorial service held for his beloved fellow-labourer in Memorial Hall. Part of the verses are as follows:

Out of the shadow-land, into the sunshine,
Cloudless, eternal, that fades not away;
Softly and tenderly Jesus will call us;
Home, were the ransomed are gath'ring today.

Out of the shadow-land, over life's ocean,
Into the rapture and joy of the Lord,
Safe in the Father's house, welcomed by angels
Ours the bright crown and eternal reward.

A singer of incomparable popularity and a composer of no small ability, Sankey found it difficult to teach others the methods that had made him so successful. This fact is to be regretted, for a pioneer in the field, with a rich and varied experience, he might have left to those song leaders and soloists who should seek to emulate him instructions of inestimable value. However, those who sought him out in his later years, to learn of him the secrets of his great success, came away disappointed. Whether he did not wish to divulge his methods, or whether he was not competent as a teacher is a matter for conjecture. It is true that Sankey was never trained for a singer and that he understood very little of the technique of music. This may account in part, for his inadequacy as a teacher. "Singing the Gospel" was his favourite expression, yet Sankey was always opposed to singing as a profession. It may be that his reticence to disclose his secrets was due to his firm conviction that gospel singing should be only in answer to divine call, and not entered into as one would choose a secular profession. Finally, it may be that God designed for Sankey a unique position in the field of evangelism, one which should never be exactly duplicated. Whatever the answer, all agree upon his irrefutable ability in "singing and making melody in his heart to the Lord."

Jesus, I will trust Thee,
Trust Thee with my soul;
Guilty, lost and helpless,
Thou canst make me whole:
There is none in heaven
Or on earth like Thee;
Thou hast died for sinners -
Therefore, Lord, for me.

Jesus, I will trust Thee;
Name of matchless worth,
Spoken by the angel
At Thy wondrous birth;
Written and for ever,
On Thy cross of shame;
Sinners read and worship,
Trusting in that Name.

Jesus, I will trust Thee,
Pondering Thy Ways;
Full of love and mercy
All Thine earthly days.
Sinners gathered round Thee,
Lepers sought Thy face;
None too vile or loathsome
For a Saviour's grace.

Jesus, I will trust Thee,
Trust without a doubt;
Whosoever cometh
Thou wilt not cast out.
Faithful is Thy promise,
Precious is Thy blood;
These my soul's salvation,
Thou my Saviour God!

7

"WHO GIVETH SONGS IN THE NIGHT"
Job 35:10

In addition to several return trips to Great Britain Ira D. Sankey also enjoyed a most delightful visit to the Holy Land. Accompanied by his wife, one of his sons and a few friends, he sailed from New York in January of 1898. After a short stop at Gibraltar the ship dropped anchor at Alexandria, Egypt. From that point travel was done by rail. The party visited all the points of general interest to tourists, including the pyramids, the Howling Dervishes, and Gizeh Museum. They also made an excursion up the historic Nile. In all, forty days where spent in the enchanting land of the Pharaohs.

Although this trip was not designed as a "singing tour", the fame of Sankey had gone before him, and again and again he was invited to sing the songs that had proclaimed his name around the world. On his first night in Cairo he went to the American Mission where he took his place among the American members of the congregation. In a few moments a missionary near him recognised the singer and expressed the desire that he would sing. A few minutes later a lady, who proved to be from Sankey's own country in Pennsylvania, pressed her way to him with the request that he sing. But there was no organ or other instrument in the hall. Undaunted, the Pennsylvania woman motioned four Egyptian soldiers out of the room, who returned promptly with a small cabinet organ. At the close of the address Sankey gave the congregation a service of sacred song, which was received with a great deal of enthusiasm and appreciation. Similar services were conducted at various points throughout Egypt, usually upon the request of missionaries who had long desired to hear the famous gospel singer. At a number of these services Sankey found that the natives were already familiar with many of his best-known songs.

In Palestine Mr. Sankey and his party visited all the points of interest so sacred to the heart of every Christian. No doubt many of the songs he had been singing for years took on a deeper significance as he stood on the very spot hallowed so many centuries before by the feet of the Master. Just outside the walls of Jerusalem Sankey stood upon a green hill and sang the noble strains of "On Calvary's Brow My Saviour Died."

In that section of Jerusalem known as Mount Zion, Sankey was delighted to find an English Bishop in charge of a fine school for children. The principal of this school proved to be an old member of Sankey's choir in London during the evangelistic campaigns of that city. Now, in their own Arabic language, the children were singing a number of Sankey's own songs. He charmed them with his rendering of "The Ninety and Nine."

On their return trip Sankey's party travelled by way of Constantinople, Athens, Naples and Rome. In these cities they visited the English, British and Scotch churches and missions, at all of which the singer was pressed into service. Everywhere it was a pleasure to learn that some of his own favourite songs were known and cherished. The man who had spent a lifetime inspiring multitudes to "sing the gospel" was already reaping the rich harvest of his own unselfish devotion to the cause of sacred song.

When he arrived in his native land once again, Sankey gave several special services of song for the soldiers stationed at Tampa, Florida. It was there that Theodore Roosevelt, then famed Colonel of the Rough Riders, invited him to visit his camp also. Sankey regretted that a previous engagement made it impossible to accept this invitation.

The following year Mr. Sankey returned once more to Great Britain, where he held special services of sacred song and story in thirty cities and towns. It was this extended engagement that impaired his health to the extent that he lost his eyesight. The sweet singer who had brought light and happiness to uncounted thousands was destined to pass the remainder of his mortal days in physical darkness. However, the hand of affliction did not touch the inner spiritual vision which always characterised his life and service. Music, always his solace and delight, now became in even deeper measure his refuge and consolation. In the strains of his own beloved hymns he found fortitude for the trying days ahead.

Of all his earthly friends who sought to bring cheer to his lonely hours none proved a greater benediction than his beloved and esteemed friend Fanny Crosby. Perhaps it was her own blindness that enabled Miss Crosby to share more fully than any other the feelings of the now stricken singer. She would often come to him, her chalice of consolation full to the brim. The two would talk over the experiences of former days. Then they would join in singing the beautiful songs which, together, they had given the world. At length, Miss Crosby would take her leave, perhaps never fully conscious of the blessing she had imparted. Mr. Sankey was left refreshed and inspired, as though an angel hand had ministered to him.

During the days of his blindness Sankey lived at his Brooklyn, New York, home, on South Oxford Street. He might have spent his last years in luxury and have left his family a handsome fortune, but he had chosen "that better part". The modest fortune, amassed from his publishing interests, was diverted to the cause of Christian education, and hundreds of worthy youth were drinking deeply at the fountains of learning, all because of his quickened vision and unselfish devotion to a loyalty that surpassed all other loyalties.

During his last five years, characterised by extreme weakness and often by excruciating pain, for glaucoma had destroyed the optic nerve, Mr. Sankey maintained a sweet spirit of Christian patience and fortitude that was a benediction to those who visited him. His mind remained clear to the end, and his sense of Christ and of heaven became increasingly real as the hour of his departure approached. It was evident that he looked forward eagerly to his heavenly reunion with Moody, his intimate association through so many happy, useful years, for he remarked, "What a meeting, what a meeting it will be!"

One friend, on taking leave of Sankey just a few weeks before the latter's death, said, "I can hardly think of Mr. Moody in heaven except as at the head of an evangelistic campaign or some other movement for Christ."

"Yes," replied Mr. Sankey, with a twinkle of merriment in his tone. "And I can hear him say: 'Come on Sankey, don't let's be late for meeting'."

The end came for Ira D. Sankey on August 13 1908, quietly, for he passed away in sleep, without a struggle. His passing caused profound sorrow, and various eminent newspapers throughout the country carried the account of his death. The Associated Press story included the following tribute:

"His voice was a baritone - clear, strong, thrilling. His own emotion vibrated through every note and set the heart of his hearers to throbbing in unison. Never was burning zeal put into more contagious and persuasive notes."

Funeral services, marked by simplicity and conducted at the LaFayette Avenue Presbyterian Church, where

Mr. Sankey held his membership during his latter years, were attended by devoted friends as well as Christian workers from far and near. At the deceased singer's own request, several of his own hymns were sung by an aged cousin of his C.C. Sankey. These included "The Ninety and Nine," "There'll be no Dark Valley," "Sleep on Beloved," and "Only Remembered." The choir of the church joined in the last number. The funeral sermon was delivered by the Rev. Dr. Charles E. Locke of Brooklyn. The Moody Bible Institute of Chicago was represented by Mr. Fitt and Mr. W. R. Moody, son of the sainted evangelist, represented the interests of Northfield.

The interment was made in Greenwood Cemetery, Brooklyn, in a beautiful spot overlooking the bay. A large block of granite, bearing the word SANKEY and a bar of music with the inscriptions "Good night" and "God is love" above and below it, marks the last earthly resting place of the beloved singer of Israel.

With a voice sweetened and tempered to heavenly chords in the crucible of human suffering, Sankey had heard the invitation to join the company of the choir invisible and immortal, there to sing forever the songs of redemption that had been his favourites here. He who had learned "songs in the night" had reached the land of fadeless day.

There'll Be No Dark Valley

There'll be no dark valley when Jesus comes,
There'll be no dark valley when Jesus comes,
There'll be no dark valley when Jesus comes
To gather His loved ones home.

To gather His loved ones home,
To gather His loved ones home;
There'll be no dark valley when Jesus comes
To gather His loved ones home.

There'll be no more sorrow when Jesus comes,
There'll be no more sorrow when Jesus comes;
But a glorious morrow when Jesus comes
To gather His loved ones home.

There'll be no more weeping when Jesus comes,
There'll be no more weeping when Jesus comes;
But a blessed reaping when Jesus comes
To gather His loved ones home.

There'll be songs of greeting when Jesus comes,
There'll be songs of greeting when Jesus comes;
And a joyful meeting when Jesus comes
To gather His loved ones home.